A QUESTRON™ ELECTRONIC WORKBOOK

MY FIRST BOOK OF MULTIPLICATION

PRICE/STERN/SLOAN
Publishers, Inc., Los Angeles

DISTRIBUTED BY
RANDOM HOUSE, INC.
New York

THE QUESTRON™ SYSTEM
COMBINING FUN WITH LEARNING

This book is part of **THE QUESTRON SYSTEM**, which offers children a unique aid to learning and endless hours of challenging entertainment.

The QUESTRON electronic "wand" uses a microchip to sense correct and incorrect answers with "right" or "wrong" sounds and lights. Victory sounds and lights reward the user when particular sets of questions or games are completed. Powered by a nine-volt alkaline battery, which is activated only when the wand is pressed on a page, QUESTRON should have an exceptionally long life. The QUESTRON ELECTRONIC WAND can be used with any book in the QUESTRON series.

A note to parents...

With QUESTRON, right or wrong answers are indicated instantly and can be tried over and over to reinforce learning and improve skills. Children need not be restricted to the books designated for their age group, as interests and rates of development vary widely. Also, within many of the books, certain pages are designed for the older end of the age group and will provide a stimulating challenge to younger children.

Many activities are designed at different levels. For example, the child can select an answer by recognizing a letter or by reading an entire word. The activities for pre-readers and early readers are intended to be used with parental assistance. Interaction with parents or older children will stimulate the learning experience.

QUESTRON Project Director: Roger Burrows
Educational Consultants: Susan Parker, Rozanne Lanczak
Writer: Beverley Dietz
Illustrator: Kathleen McCarthy
Graphic Designers: Judy Walker, Lee A. Scott

Copyright ©1985 by Price/Stern/Sloan Publishers, Inc. All rights reserved under International and Pan-American Copyright Conventions. No part of this publication may be reproduced, stored in a retrieval system, or transmitted in any form or by any means, electronic, mechanical, photocopying, recording or otherwise, without the prior written permission of the publisher. Published by Price/Stern/Sloan Publishers, Inc., 410 North La Cienega Boulevard, Los Angeles, California 90048. Distributed by Random House, Inc., 201 East 50th Street, New York, New York 10022.   ISBN: 0-394-87706-3

2 3 4 5 6 7 8 9 0

Printed in the United States of America
QUESTRON™ is a trademark of Price/Stern/Sloan Publishers, Inc.
U.S.A. and International Patents Pending

HOW TO START QUESTRON

Hold **QUESTRON** at this angle and press the activator button firmly on the page.

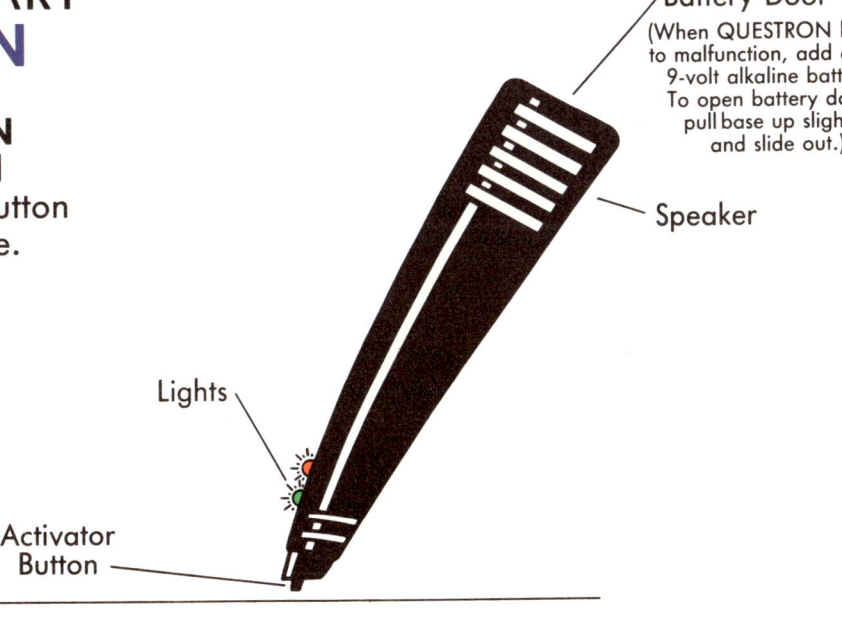

HOW TO USE QUESTRON

PRESS
Press **QUESTRON** firmly on the shape below, then lift it off.

TRACK
Press **QUESTRON** down on "Start" and keep it pressed down as you move to "Finish."

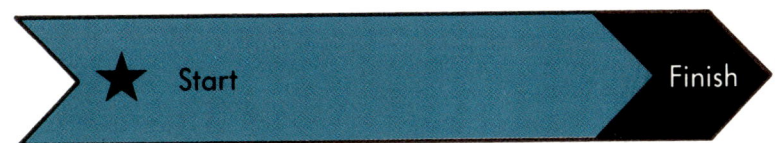

RIGHT & WRONG WITH QUESTRON

Press **QUESTRON** on the square.

See the green light and hear the sound. This green light and sound say "You are correct."

Press **QUESTRON** on the triangle.

The red light and sound say "Try again." Lift **QUESTRON** off the page and wait for the sound to stop.

Press **QUESTRON** on the circle.

Hear the victory sound. Don't be dazzled by the flashing lights. You deserve them.

Bicycle Fun

Two people ride on each bike. Look at each picture.
How many bikes are there? How many people are there all together?
Press **Questron** on the correct answer to each question.

How many bikes?

How many people in all?

How many bikes?

How many people in all?

How many bikes?

How many people in all?

Skill: Multiplying 2's

How many bikes?

How many people in all?

How many bikes?

How many people in all?

How many bikes?

How many people in all?

The Toy Store

Three toys sit on each shelf. Look at each picture. How many shelves of toys are there? How many toys are there all together? Press **Questron** on the correct answer to each question.

How many shelves?

How many piggy banks in all?

How many shelves?

How many dolls in all?

How many shelves?

How many ducks in all?

Skill: Multiplying 3's

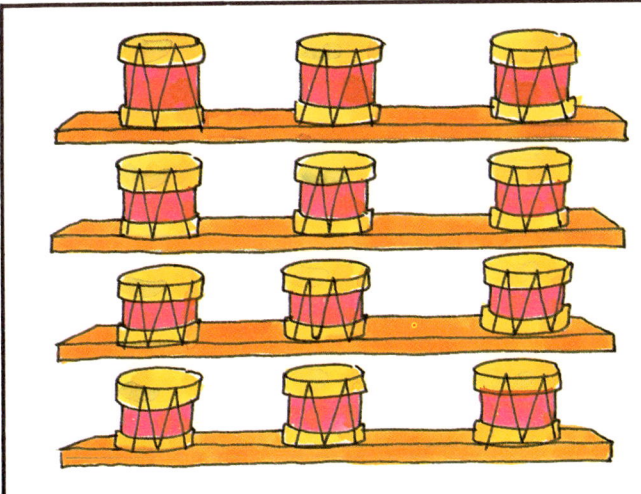

How many shelves?

How many drums in all?
 12

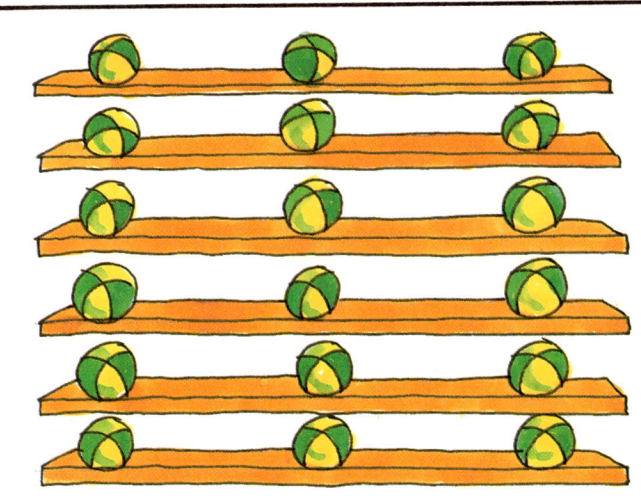

How many shelves?

How many balls in all?

How many shelves?

How many trucks in all?

Castle Climb

Help the hikers climb the castle wall.
Track **Questron** on the multiples of **2**. Start on the ★.

Skill: Identifying multiples of 2

Fruit Salad

Four pieces of fruit are on each plate. Look at each picture. How many plates of fruit are there? How many pieces of fruit all together? Press **Questron** on the correct answer to each question.

How many plates?

How many pears in all?

How many plates?

How many oranges in all?

How many plates?

How many plums in all?

Skill: Multiplying 4's

How many plates?

How many cherries in all?

How many plates?

How many apples in all?

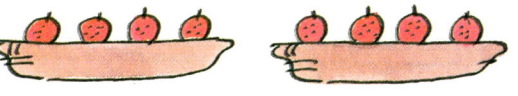

How many plates?

How many strawberries in all?

A Bird's-Eye View

Press **Questron** on the number sentence that goes with each picture.

Skill: Multiplying 1, 2, 3, 4 and 5 / Recognizing number sentences

Time to Move

Press **Questron** on the correct answers.

2 × 3 = 5 6 8

3 × 3 = 6 8 9

1 × 4 = 1 4 8

2 × 5 = 5 10 15

Skill: Completing number sentences

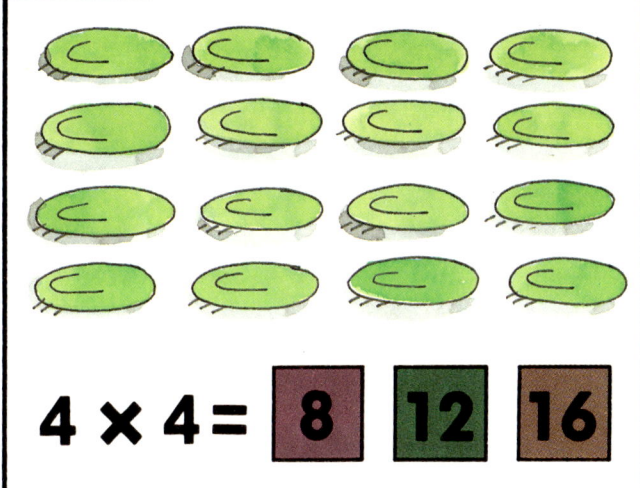

4 × 4 = 8 12 16

1 × 3 = 1 3 6

2 × 4 = 2 4 8

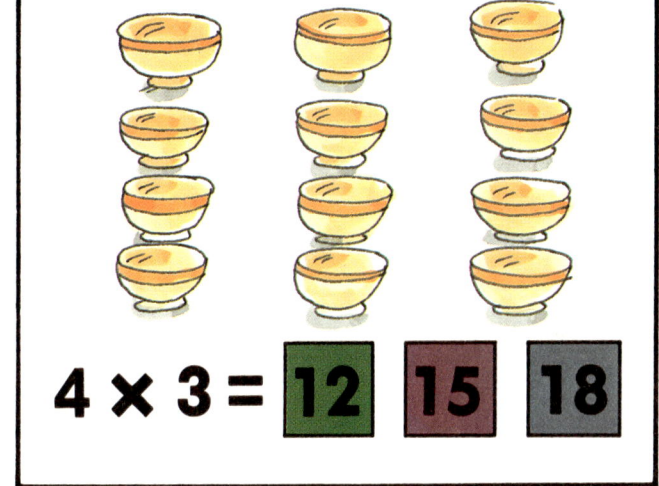

4 × 3 = 12 15 18

Space Race

Track **Questron** on the path that has the correct number sentences. Start on the ★.

2 × 5 = 7

2 × 5 = 10

3 × 3 = 9

3 × 3 = 10

4 × 6 = 20

4 × 6 = 24

1 × 4 = 5

1 × 4 = 4

Skill: Identifying correct number sentences

Can You Canoe?

Five people sit in each canoe. How many canoes are there next to each dock? How many people are there all together? Track **Questron** to the correct answer to each number sentence. Start on the ★.

Skill: Multiplying 5's

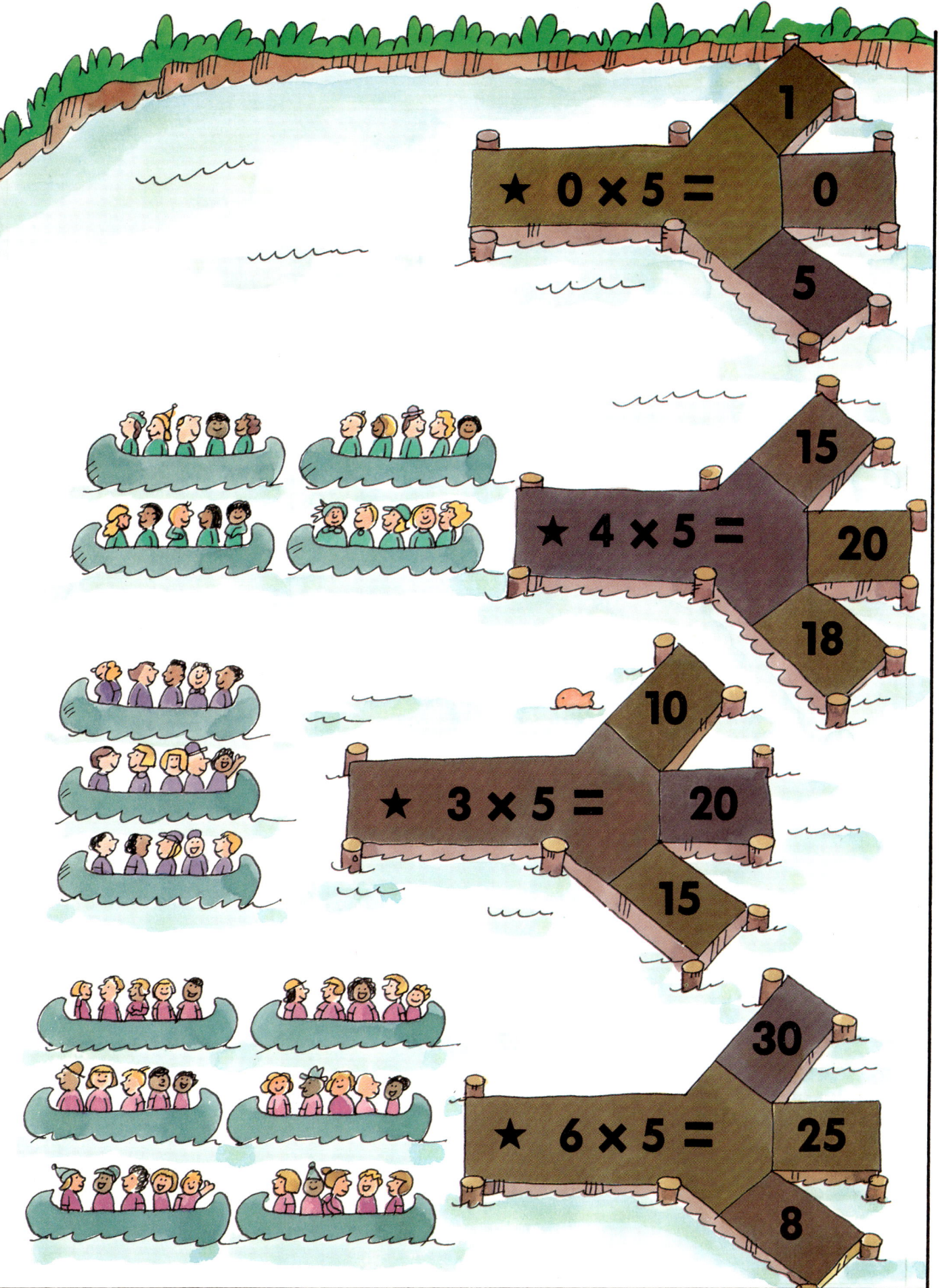

Heavy Weights

Six weights are on each barbell. Look at each picture. How many barbells are there? How many weights are there all together?
Press **Questron** on the answer to each number sentence.

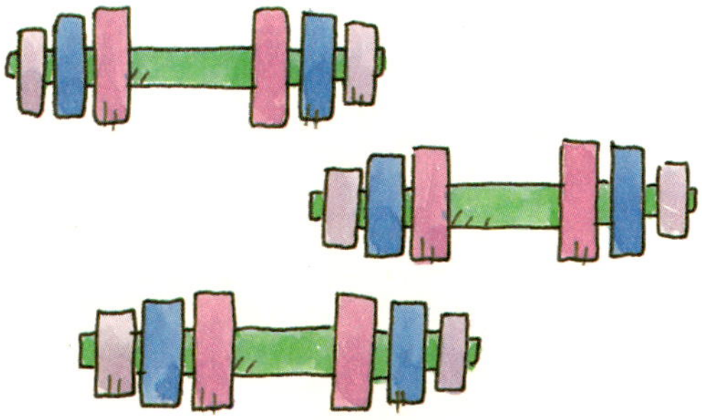

3 × 6 = 9 18 20

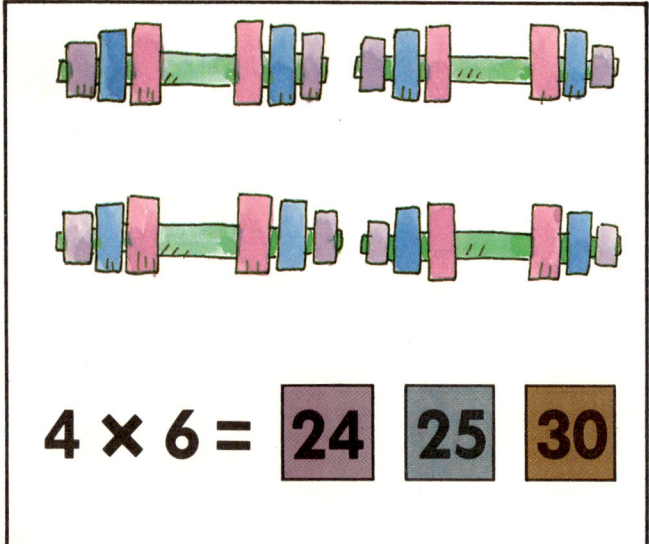

4 × 6 = 24 25 30

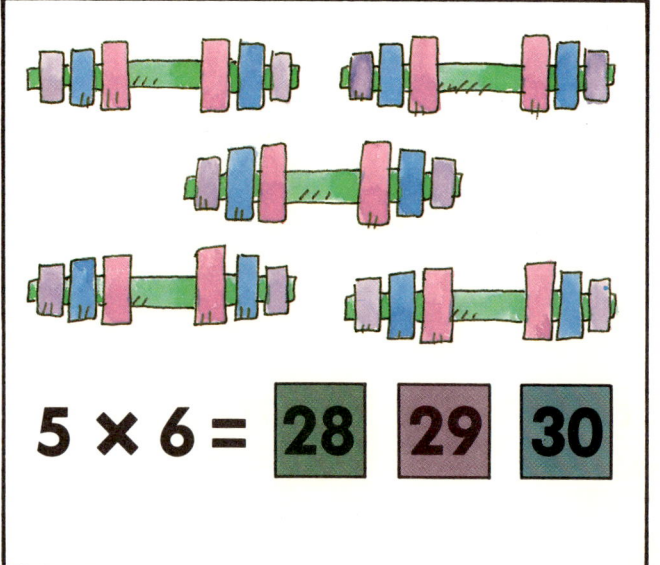

5 × 6 = 28 29 30

Skill: Multiplying 6's

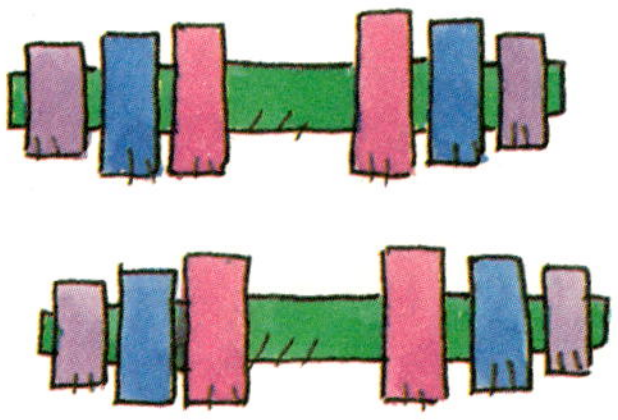

2 × 6 = 8 10 **12**

1 × 6 = **6** 7 ~~1~~

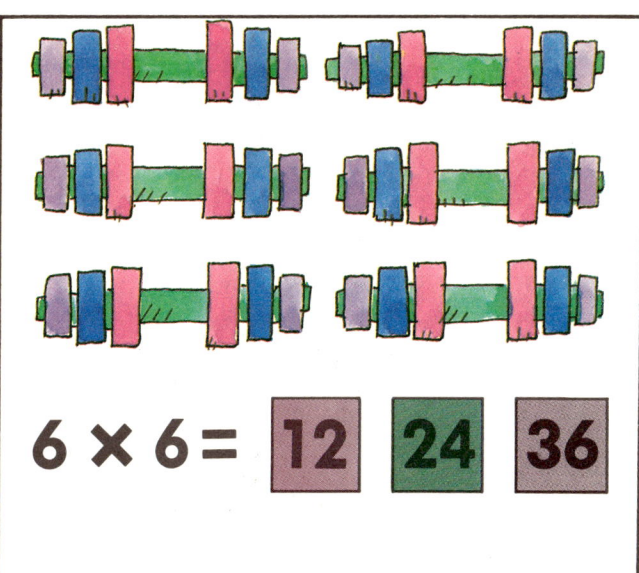

6 × 6 = 12 24 **36**

Clowning Around

How many balloons is each clown holding? Press **Questron** on the correct number sentence next to each clown.

Skill: Solving multiplication problems

Shooting Baskets

Look at the number on each basket. Only multiplication problems with answers that match that number belong in the basket.
Press **Questron** on the balls that belong in the basket.

Skill: Recognizing the commutative property of multiplication problems

Robot Race

Track **Questron** on the correct numbers. Start on the ★.

Skill: Identifying multiples of 4, 5, and 6

Number Crunch

Track **Questron** on the multiplication problems with correct answers. Start on the ★.

★						
2×2=4	5×5=25	2×5=8	3×6=12	6×6=35	5×4=18	5×5=24
0×2=2	6×3=18	1×1=2	6×6=36	4×5=20	2×1=2	4×5=18
4×2=8	1×3=3	5×1=6	2×3=6	6×5=21	6×4=24	5×4=30
6×1=6	3×4=7	4×4=16	2×5=10	5×3=16	5×6=30	3×3=8
5×4=20	2×2=5	2×4=8	6×0=6	5×2=10	7×3=21	6×6=35
7×3=21	4×4=18	3×3=9	1×4=5	8×2=16	5×5=26	8×3=22
3×4=12	3×2=6	1×5=5	3×4=13	6×6=36	4×6=24	3×6=18

Skill: Solving multiplication problems

Working Out

Press **Questron** on the correct answers.

Pablo walks 4 miles every day.

How far does he walk in 3 days?

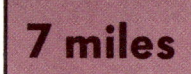
7 miles 10 miles 12 miles

Jean swims 2 miles every day.

How far does she swim in 5 days?

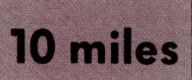
10 miles 12 miles 15 miles

Lily runs 1 mile every day.

How far does she run in 6 days?

1 mile 6 miles 7 miles

Tom rides 3 miles every day.

How far does he ride in 4 days?

7 miles 12 miles 16 miles

Skill: Solving word problems

Sue jogs 3 miles every day.

How far does she jog in 5 days?

| 8 miles | 10 miles | 15 miles |

Tina rides 6 miles every day.

How far does she ride in 5 days?

| 20 miles | 25 miles | 30 miles |

Jeff skates 2 miles every day.

How far does he skate in 2 days?

| 3 miles | 4 miles | 6 miles |

Tony hikes 4 miles every day.

How far does he hike in 5 days?

| 20 miles | 24 miles | 30 miles |

Surprise Package

Press **Questron** on the correct answers.

Roger has 3 boxes.

4 presents are in each box.

How many presents in all?

Katy has 4 boxes.

4 presents are in each box.

How many presents in all?

Lisa has 6 boxes.

1 present is in each box.

How many presents in all?

Sam has 5 boxes.

5 presents are in each box.

How many presents in all?

Skill: Solving word problems

Jerry has 2 boxes.

6 presents are in each box.

How many presents in all?

Nick has 3 boxes.

5 presents are in each box.

How many presents in all?

Rosa has 5 boxes.

4 presents are in each box.

How many presents in all?

Nora has 3 boxes.

3 presents are in each box.

How many presents in all?

THE QUESTRON LIBRARY OF ELECTRONIC BOOKS

A series of books specially designed to
reach—and teach—and entertain children of all ages

QUESTRON ELECTRONIC WORKBOOKS

Early Childhood

My First Counting Book
My First ABC Book
My First Book of Animals
Shapes and Sizes
Preschool Skills
My First Vocabulary
My First Nursery Rhymes
Reading Readiness
My First Words
My First Numbers
Going Places
Kindergarten Skills
Sesame Street® 1 to 10
Sesame Street® A to Z
Autos, Ships, Trains and Planes

Grades K–5

My First Reading Book (K–1)
Little Miss™ — First School Days (K–2)
Mr. Men™ — A First Reading Adventure (K–2)
Word Games (K–2)
My First Book of Telling Time (K–2)
Day of the Dinosaur (K–3)
First Grade Skills (1)
My First Book of Addition (1–2)
Bigger, Smaller, Shorter, Taller... (1–3)
The Storytime Activity Book (1–3)
My Robot Book (1–3)
My First Book of Spelling (1–3)
My First Book of Subtraction (1–3)
My First Book of Multiplication (2–3)
I Want to Be... (2–5)
Number Fun (2–5)
Word Fun (2–5)

Electronic Quizbooks for the Whole Family

Trivia Fun and Games
How, Why, Where and When
More How, Why, Where and When
World Records and Amazing Facts

The Princeton Review S.A.T.® Program

The Princeton Review: S.A.T.® Math
The Princeton Review: S.A.T.® Verbal

PRICE/STERN/SLOAN — **RANDOM HOUSE, INC.**
Publishers, Inc., Los Angeles   New York

GP9/86